Sam Walshaw

Maisey and the Pirates
The Ghost Ship

The four pesky pirates had received word
of a great hoard of real pirate treasure!

"Ahhrrrr," said Captain Codeye,
frantically thumbing through his pirate book!
"I have read all about the infamous treasure
of Captain Pinkbeard.
She was the most fearsome girl pirate
ever to have sailed the seven seas."

The pirates listened intensely as Captain Codeye
told them the story of Pinkbeard,
and how she still roams the seven seas
in her ghost ship, haunting the ships of
any pirate who would try to steal her treasure!

The pirates didn't believe in ghosts,
but they did believe in treasure!

"Ahhrrrr"
yelled the crew...
"What are we waiting for, lets go!"

Milly, who was Maiseys little sister, had been listening to the pirates talking about their forthcoming adventure.

"CAN I COME, Pleeeeeease!?" begged Milly!

"No, sorry!" said Maisey,
"A big voyage like this is only
for BIG pirates, and you are definitely
NOT a big pirate!"

"Ohhh," said Milly!
But Milly wasn't going to take no
for an answer—she had
a plan of her own!

As the pirates sailed, they talked about
Pinkbeard's treasure.

"I wonder what the treasure will be?" said Daisy,
"I bet it's diamonds!" said Maisey
"I think it's gold" said Kearan!

The pirates were working hard aboard ship,
so Daisy decided she would make them
a midnight snack to keep them going
until morning!
(As this was going to be a long voyage!)

In the galley, Daisy prepared
jam sandwiches and milk
for all the pirates,
as this was their favorite
midnight snack!

As Daisy turned around, she saw
a ghostly figure floating past the door!

"Ahhhhhhhhhhhh," screamed Daisy,
dropping the sandwiches and milk,
as she ran as fast as she could
back to the other pirates.

"What's wrong Daisy?" asked Kearan
"I s-s-saw the ghost" said Daisey,
"the ghost of Pinkbeard,
sh-sh-she was in the galley!"

"Don't be silly, Daisy. There are
no such things as ghosts!" laughed Kearan.

"BUT I DID! I did see something,
she was definitely there!" said Daisy.

"Hmmm......
maybe I will just check."
thought Kearan!
He climbed up to his crows nest,
just to make sure there was no sign
of Pinkbeard, and her ghost ship!

As Kearan peered through his
telescope he heard a strange noise!
"Whooooo.. Whooooo...."
"WHATS THAT!" thought Kearan!
Then he felt an icy hand on
the back of his neck!

frozen
peas

Kearan didn't dare look back, as
he ran back down to the other pirates,
to tell them what had happened!

"She's here!" said Kearan, his voice trembling!
"Who's here?" said Captain Codeye?
"Th-th-the ghost...th-th-the ghost of Pinkbeard!"
"Don't be silly, Kearan, you know there are no
such thing as ghosts!" said Captain Codeye.
"BUT DAISY SAW HER TOO!" said Kearan.

"Hmmmm," thought Captain Codeye.
He took his flashlight,
and went to investigate!

Captain Codeye walked to the bow of the ship, when suddenly a ghostly figure appeared right in front of him!

"Ahhhhhhhhhhhhhhh!" screamed Captain Codeye. He ran, as fast as he could, back to the pirates! "I-I-I think the ghost of Pinkbeard is real!!"

"What's going on?" said Maisey.
"What's all the shouting about?"

"Sh-sh-she is here, we have all seen her,
the ghost of Pinkbeard....she is on our ship!"

Just then Maisey spotted something laying on the deck. "What's that?" asked Daisy. "Hmmm, its Milly's head scalf," said Maisey "I think I know what could be happening here! I have a plan!" whispered Maisey.

"Shhhhhhhh" said Maisey, "look there she is!"
The pirates crept up to where Milly was hiding!

"BOO!" shouted all the pirates.
Milly nearly jumped out of her skin!

"Ohhhh, please don't get me ghost pirates,
I won't steel your treasure, I promise I won't!
I'm only a tiny little pirate!"

All the pirates burst out laughing!
"THAT WAS NOT FUNNY!" said Milly, sulking!
The pirates decide they would go home, they had
had enough adventure for one night!

"BUT WAIT, LOOK" said Milly,
"it's true, there is a ghost ship, look!"

"MILLY!!!"....said the pirates, "don't be silly
we are not falling for that one again!"

The pirates sailed home to get some sleep,
ready for another big adventure!

"Good bye!"

Sam Walshaw

Maisey and the Pirates
Ghost Ship

Maisey and her friends delight
in another Piratey adventure!
But something scary
is lurking about the ship!
What could it be?

ISBN 978-1-906081-99-7

9 781906 081997 >

Albury Children's
www.alburybooks.com/childrens

RRP £6.99

Albury Books

rockpool
children's books